Fact Finders®

MEDIA LITERACY

TV TAKEOVER

Questioning Television

by Guofang Wan

Capstone
press®

Mankato, Minnesota

Fact Finders is published by Capstone Press,
151 Good Counsel Drive, P.O. Box 669, Mankato, Minnesota 56002.
www.capstonepub.com

032010
5713R

Library of Congress Cataloging-in-Publication Data
Wan, Guofang.
    TV takeover : questioning television/by Guofang Wan.
    p. cm.—(Fact Finders. Media literacy)
    Summary: "Describes what media is, how television is part of media, and encourages readers to
question the medium's influential messages"—Provided by publisher.
    Includes bibliographical references and index.
    ISBN-13: 978-0-7368-6763-4 (hardcover)
    ISBN-10: 0-7368-6763-5 (hardcover)
    ISBN-13: 978-0-7368-7859-3 (softcover pbk.)
    ISBN-10: 0-7368-7859-9 (softcover pbk.)
    1. Television broadcasting—Juvenile literature. I. Title. II. Series.
PN1992.57.W36 2007
384.55—dc22   2006021442

Editorial Credits
Jennifer Besel, editor; Juliette Peters, designer; Jo Miller, photo researcher/photo editor

Photo Credits
Bulova Corporation, 28 (commercial)
Capstone Press/Karon Dubke, 4 (all), 7 (all), 13, 14, 17 (*Lizzie McGuire*), 18 (all), 19, 20, 23, 24 (all), 25, 26
    (all), 27 (fade images), 29 (all)
Capstone Press/TJ Thoraldson Digital Photography, 10 (all), 11 (all)
Corbis/Bettmann, 28 (Philo Farnsworth)
Courtesy of Guofang Wan, 32
Getty Images Inc./Stone+/Gregg Segal, 27
PhotoEdit Inc./Michael Newman, 12
Shutterstock/J. Helgason, cover (static); Ken Hurst, cover (TV); Melissa King, cover (remote control)
Supplied by Capital Pictures, 8, 9 (*24*), 22
The Kobal Collection/CTW/Jim Henson Prod., 16; NBC-TV, 17 (*The Office*); Trump Prod./Mark Burnett
    Prod., 9 (*The Apprentice*); Warner Bros TV, 6; Warner Bros. TV/Chuck Lorre Prod., 9 (*Two and a Half Men*)
Zuma Press/Copyright 2004 by Cosima Scavolini/La Presse, 15; Copyright 2005 by Courtesy Ford, 21

The author would like to thank Jami Paintiff for her assistance in preparing this book.

TABLE OF CONTENTS

Can you imagine what life would be like without TV? No up-to-the-minute news coverage. No sports. No *Simpsons*, *American Idol*, or *CSI*. Where would we get all our information?

TV is part of the **media**. Video games, movies, and the Internet are all part of the media too. As you can see, the media plays a big role in our lives. It gives us entertainment and information. It also gives us ideas. And those ideas can **influence** our thoughts and decisions.

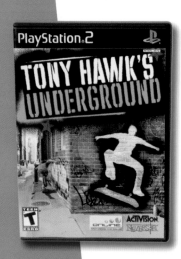

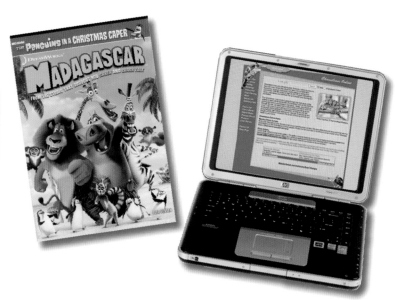

TV stations and advertisers know just how influenced we can be. That's why it's good to question those TV messages. Here are some questions to help get you started.

QUESTION IT!

Who made the message and why?

Who is the message for?

How might others view the message differently?

What is left out of the message?

How does the message get and keep my attention?

INSIDE TV

Who made the message and why?

TV is a money-making business. Sure, we get entertainment and information, but the real purpose of this biz is to bring in the cash. Networks make all their money by selling airtime to advertisers. But there's a catch. Advertisers want to get the most for their money. So they advertise when the most people are watching. Hit shows like *The OC* bring in lots of viewers for FOX. FOX can then charge advertisers more to play commercials during those shows.

The race to get viewers is pretty competitive. If a show doesn't bring in the viewers, you won't see it in *TV Guide* anymore. It's cancelled.

The more viewers *The OC* brings in, the more FOX can charge for advertising time during the show.

LINGO

airtime: time during a network's programming

network: a central company that sends out programming to TV stations across the country

REALITY CHECK

When is 30 seconds of airtime worth $2.5 million? When it's during the Super Bowl! In 2006, ABC charged advertisers $2.5 million to air one 30-second commercial during the game. Why would advertisers spend so much? The Super Bowl is a rare television event that draws in more than 85 million viewers. Since the Super Bowl is known for good commercials, many of those viewers are actually watching the ads. That makes the time worth the cost.

Super Bowl ads are often hilarious. Do you think using humor helps to sell a product?

More Ads Comin' Up

In this age of TiVo and DVRs, viewers can skip right over commercials. That has advertisers looking for new ways to get your attention. Their answer: product placement. On *American Idol*, do you think that Simon, Paula, and Randy really like Coca-Cola that much? Probably not. Coke just paid producers a ton of money to place their logo in the show. Next time you watch a show, see if you can find some product placements there too.

Yo, dog. Do you look at those Coke glasses just a little differently now?

CAN YOU SPOT THE AD?

You might be surprised by how many product placements are in the shows you watch. Take a look at these images from TV shows. Can you spot the ad?

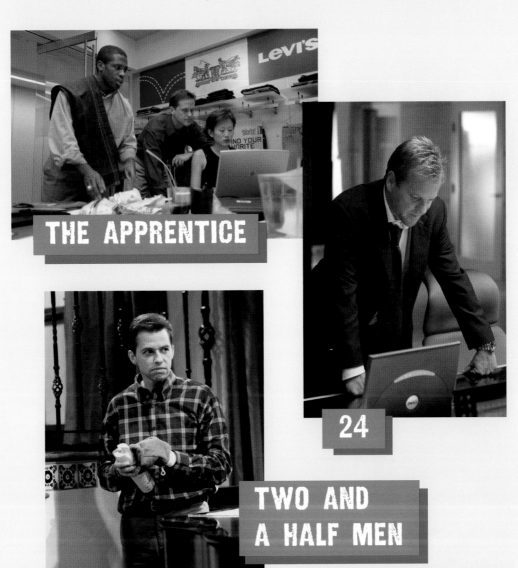

THE APPRENTICE

24

TWO AND A HALF MEN

Advertisers wouldn't have anybody watching their commercials if it weren't for the shows. It takes all kinds of people to get programs on the air. Here's a look at who's making the shows you watch.

The **PRODUCER** is the master controller. She creates programs and hires the rest of the team.

The **SCRIPTWRITER** writes the stories that the actors perform.

The **DIRECTOR** is the boss of the control room. He tells the actors and camera operators what to do in the studio.

The **CAMERA OPERATOR** works with the cameras. He films the action you'll see on the screen.

The **ACTOR** does just what her name says: act. Actors are the people you see on the screen.

The **EDITOR** selects, shortens, and rearranges the scenes.

Who is the message for?

When it comes right down to it, the goal of TV commercials (and product placements) is to influence you. Advertisers want to get people to buy what they are selling. But advertisers don't **market** to just anybody. They are very specific about who they are selling to.

Take a look at this marketing **slogan**: "Silly rabbit! Trix are for kids!" Can you guess who they're targeting?

Do you think a commercial showing older actors would be trying to sell a product to you?

Commercials that target kids air during shows kids watch. Tons of cereal and toy commercials run during Saturday morning cartoons. The same idea is true for commercials targeting men, women, or the elderly. You don't usually see a commercial for AARP (American Association of Retired Persons) during *Yu-Gi-Oh!*

LINGO

air: to put a show on TV

A Station for Me

TV networks know they can make more money if they can offer advertisers a better way to reach their target audiences. So, many cable channels offer programming to interest certain groups of people. This is called narrowcasting. And advertisers love it.

Nickelodeon, for example, targets kids by playing only shows like *SpongeBob SquarePants*.

LINGO

narrowcasting: airing shows that appeal to certain groups

target audience: the group of people that producers think will be interested in the message the show is sending

Advertisers looking to sell products to kids will spend a lot of money to get their commercials on a channel like Nickelodeon.

Other cable channels like MTV, The History Channel, and Food Network are also examples of narrowcasting. These stations know that only certain people will be interested in the shows on their channel. And so do advertisers.

TRY IT OUT!

Networks create shows so advertisers will want to spend money on commercials. Your job is to create a new show to attract advertisers. Grab a notebook and a pencil. Write up who the characters in your show would be, how long the show would be, and an outline for the pilot. Answer these questions as you're planning your new show.

- Who is your show for?
- What would your show be about?
- What companies would be interested in advertising during your show?

Who the show is for:
Kids like me

What the show is about:
A cat that can talk to her human owner.

Characters:
Murphy - a black and white cat
Julie - a 10 year old girl who can understand what her cat is saying
Linda - Julie's mom
Jen - Julie's best friend. Jen can't understand Murphy, so she thinks her friend is a little crazy. Nobody knows about Julie's ability except Jen.

Outline for the pilot:
Starts on a warm summer day.

15

Stay Tuned for Values

How might others view the message differently?

TV isn't one-size-fits-all. Even though one show is popular, it doesn't mean everyone in the world likes it. But why is that the case? Well, it's all about what we think is important. It's about values. Age, gender, life experiences, and even religious beliefs factor into our values. They help us decide what's funny, what's mean, and what's true.

Sesame Street was probably one of your favorite shows a few years ago. But as your values changed, so did your taste in TV shows.

Trash or Treasure?

Think about what you see on TV now. Some people find the show *The Office* hilarious. But others don't find it funny at all. Kids totally get the *Lizzie McGuire* show. But parents think the show is lame. What one person thinks is a great **spoof** could be **offensive** to someone else. Nobody has exactly the same values.

Do you think TV producers look at their target audience's values to decide what things to talk about in a show? You bet. Topics on the *Lizzie McGuire* show won't be the same as topics on *The Office*. Their audiences value different things.

On *Friends*, Rachel gave Joey a Ralph Lauren shirt. You can bet it was an ad to sell us the brand name.

What Should I Think Today?

Values on TV can influence how we look, act, or feel. When characters wear name-brand clothes, they're trying to sell us the label. Commercials want you to think you'll be able to do amazing things if you use their products.

© 2005. The Coca-Cola Company. "VAULT", the VAULT logo and "Get to it" are trademarks of The Coca-Cola Company.

If you drink this beverage you might be moved to create your own sports field, just like the man in this commercial. Or maybe not!

Stereotypes are a value TV shows **promote**. Stock characters give an overly simple view of a type of person. You've seen them. The nerdy smart kid. The not-so-smart blonde. The street-wise black friend. Values on TV aren't necessarily bad. TV is a great place to get ideas. But when we start believing that all smart people are dorks, then we've got a problem.

LINGO

stock character: a type of character that is used in TV shows

What kind of stock characters do they use in *Malcolm in the Middle*?

TRY IT OUT!

Write a script about a day in your life. Make your parents, friends, or even your dog characters in your show. (Don't forget to include yourself!) Give your characters dialogue that promotes your values. Here are some questions to help get you started.

- What do you believe in very strongly?
- What do you love?
- What do you hate?
- What is really important to you?

Mom: Adam! What are you doing?

Adam: I'm doing what I love most in the world—cleaning my room.

Dad: I thought you hated cleaning your room?

Adam: No, Dad. I hate brushing my teeth. Having a clean room is what I love.

Sister: The Simpsons are on TV, Adam.

Adam: That's OK. I have to go help grandma mow her lawn first. That's more important to me.

When you have your script written, have some friends help you act out your show. See if your friends can pick out your values.

What is left out of the message?

Before the 1970s, tobacco companies used commercials to convince people to smoke. But what didn't their commercials tell us? Well, they didn't say how addictive cigarettes are. They didn't say that smoking is a health risk either. But because viewers weren't given all the info, many were influenced to smoke.

Tobacco companies even used cartoon characters to sell their products. Who do you think their target audience was?

You see, commercials sometimes leave info out. Why do they do that? Because they want to make their product look good. Toy commercials leave out that the toy will break if you drop it. Car commercials leave out bad results on a safety test. If the commercials had told all the bad stuff, do you think many people would have bought what the ad was selling?

In 2006, the Ford Fusion got some poor safety ratings. Do you think they mentioned that in their ads?

TRY IT OUT!

With a group of friends, write a commercial that highlights all the bad things about a product. You could make a commercial talking about cereal that tastes like dirt or makeup that stains your face. When you are done, act out your commercial. Then answer these questions.

- Would anyone pay attention to your ad? Why or why not?
- Would people want to buy the product you are selling? Why or why not?

This make-up is great! It stains your eyes a bright orange.

Yeah! It smells really gross too. Kind of like B.O.

It's on sale now at a store near you.

It's priced so low you can buy it with only a year's worth of allowance money!

We get to watch the survivors for only one hour each week. Have you ever wondered about what we're not shown?

Missing Pieces

Have you ever noticed that reality shows like *Survivor* are really dramatic? That's because the boring stuff was all **edited** out. We don't usually see the players having day-to-day conversations. But we're always there for the fights. Wonder why? Fights are more exciting. That's why we have to question what we're shown. Reality TV might not be reality after all.

REALITY CHECK

In April 2006, U.S. news broadcasts headlined that crude oil prices had risen to $70 per barrel. The newscasts stated that this price set a record for the highest price ever. This was true. No one had ever paid $70 per barrel before. But what viewers weren't told was that if **inflation** was taken into account, the $70 per barrel wasn't really a record. You see, in January 1981, a barrel of oil cost $38.85. According to the U.S. Energy Administration, that is equal to $86.99 today. The news stories weren't wrong when they said *paying* $70 per barrel was a record. They just misled viewers to believe that prices had never been higher. Sometimes information is left out of news reports too. That's why we even have to question the news.

TRICKS OF THEIR TRADE

How does the message get my attention?

Networks have a tough job getting us to sit down and watch their shows (and commercials). One way to get viewers is to play commercials promoting shows. But these aren't just plain old commercials. These are fast-paced, action-packed whirlwinds of information. Marketers use quick cuts to piece together a summary of a show. Have you ever watched a show because the preview looked great, only to find that it wasn't quite so exciting?

Lost is an exciting show. But next time you see a commercial for it, pay attention to how many quick cuts they use to make you excited.

LINGO

quick cut: fast scene changes that are meant to jolt and excite you

24

Watch and Win!

    With so many programs to choose from on
TV, marketers have to find other ways to get us to
watch. Some shows offer cash prizes to viewers. Those
features aren't there just as an added bonus. They are
there to influence you to watch. *Wheel of Fortune* has a
club you can join. If they roll your number during the
show, you win a prize. But you have to be watching to
see if your number comes up.

How does the message keep my attention?

On the screen, a car races down a street. Suddenly, you are face-to-face with the car as it heads straight for you. This is a trick. A trick of the TV-show-making system. Cutaway shots make us feel like we're right in the action. Cutaways, as well as tracking shots and fades, are only a few of the tricks shows use to boost their jolts per minute.

LINGO

cutaway: a quick change in the angle of the camera that brings the viewer face-to-face with the action

jolts per minute: scene changes that happen very quickly or very often in order to keep viewers interested and excited

Fade Away

You're watching a scene and slowly the image begins to disappear. The fade is a dramatic effect TV shows use to end a scene.

Track 'em Down

A show would get boring if you couldn't see the action. Tracking shots are a trick camera operators use to keep you in the moment. The camera and the operator ride on a truck, wheelchair, or a cart on a track. They stay focused on the subject by moving along with it.

Tune In Next Time

TV is great fun. It's also a great influence. Next time you sit down to watch your favorite shows, tune in these questions too. You might be surprised by what you see. Happy watching!

TIME LINE

Philo T. Farnsworth applies for a patent on the image dissector tube, beginning the age of electronic TV.

The first TV commercial airs.

1927   **1928**   **1941**   **1948**

The Federal Communications Commission (FCC) issues the first TV license to W3XK.

Cable TV begins

The FCC begins requiring TV broadcasts to post ratings on the content of each show.

News broadcasts headline record oil prices, but leave out some information.

1971 **1997** *JAN. 2006* *APRIL 2006*

TV advertising of tobacco products is banned.

ABC charges $2.5 million for a 30-second spot during Super Bowl XL, showing how much advertisers will pay to get their products in front of a lot of viewers.

GLOSSARY

edit (ED-it)—to cut and rearrange pieces of film to make a movie or television program

inflation (in-FLAY-shuhn)—an increase in prices

influence (IN-floo-uhnss)—to have an effect on someone or something

market (MAR-kit)—to sell

media (MEE-dee-uh)—a group of mediums that communicates messages; one piece of the media, like television, is called a medium.

offensive (uh-FEN-siv)—causing anger or hurt feelings

promote (pruh-MOTE)—to make the public aware of something or someone

slogan (SLOH-guhn)—a phrase or motto used by a business, a group, or an individual

spoof (SPOOF)—a funny imitation of something

INTERNET SITES

FactHound offers a safe, fun way to find Internet sites related to this book. All of the sites on FactHound have been researched by our staff.

Here's how:

1. Visit *www.facthound.com*

2. Choose your grade level.

3. Type in this book ID **0736867635** for age-appropriate sites. You may also browse subjects by clicking on letters, or by clicking on pictures and words.

4. Click on the **Fetch It** button.

FactHound will fetch the best sites for you!

READ MORE

Ali, Dominic. *Media Madness: An Insider's Guide to Media*. Tonawanda, N.Y.: Kids Can Press, 2005.

Chambers, Catherine. *Television*. Behind Media. Chicago: Heinemann, 2001.

Pelusey, Michael, and Jane Pelusey. *Film and Television*. The Media. Philadelphia: Chelsea House, 2005.

INDEX

MEET THE AUTHOR

Dr. Guofang Wan teaches future teachers at Ohio University. She is a big fan of teaching children with and about multimedia. Her other book, *The Media-Savvy Student*, and her many journal articles help to bring media literacy into the classroom.